T0397879

HOW TO BUILD OUR WORLD

FUSION

Design a
DESERT

By William Anthony

BEARPORT
PUBLISHING

Minneapolis, Minnesota

Credits

Cover – Pogorelova Olga, Magicleaf, Patrick Poendl, Anton Petrus, Ondrej Prosicky, Tarikdiz, Kumeko, curiosity. 4–5 – schallerimages, Christopher Wood. 6–7 – Panda Vector, Anton Petrus. 8–9 – Claudia Pylinskaya, Nikolai Zaburdaev, hermitis, Prystai. 10–11 – JulezHohlfeld, Orlov Sergei. 12–13 – SHUTTPHOTO, Anna Zubar. 14–15 – VikiVector, Kenneth Keifer, Alex Lerner. 16–17 – Ali A Suliman, PeterD_SA, Roger de Montfort, GoodStudio, Svetsol, Emilia K, Katflare. 18–19 – SKvector, Patrick Poendl, mario.bono. 20–21 – nickolai_self_taught, Regina F. Silva, SunshineVector, vladsilver, FloridaStock. 22–23 – frozenbunn, nikiteev_konstantin, zizi_mentos, Anna Frajtova.

Library of Congress Cataloging-in-Publication Data is available at www.loc.gov or upon request from the publisher.

ISBN: 978-1-63691-920-1 (hardcover)
ISBN: 978-1-63691-926-3 (paperback)
ISBN: 978-1-63691-932-4 (ebook)

© 2023 Booklife Publishing
This edition is published by arrangement with Booklife Publishing.

For more information, write to Bearport Publishing, 5357 Penn Avenue South, Minneapolis, MN 55419. Printed in the United States of America.

Contents

How to Build Our World

Our world is wonderful. It is full of places to go and things to see. There are different **environments**, from mountains to deserts. Each one has plants, animals, and more.

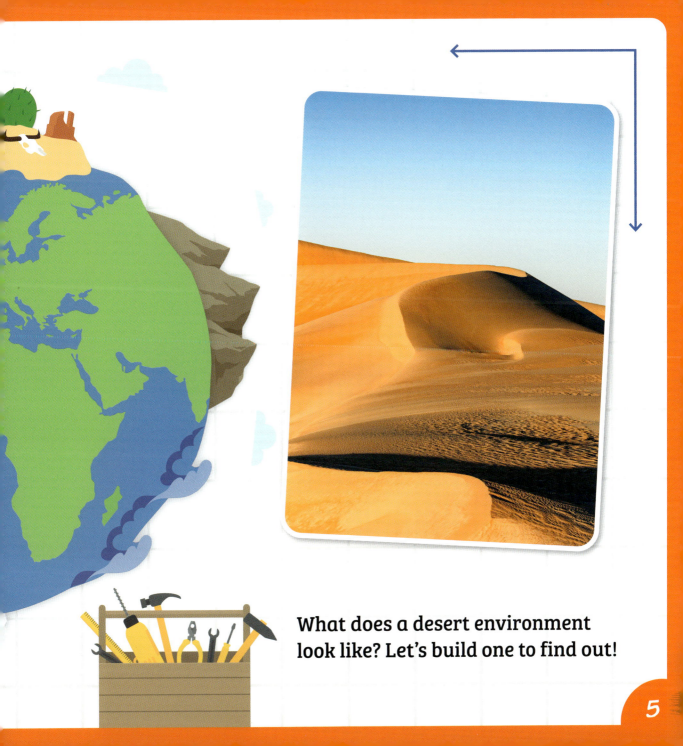

What does a desert environment look like? Let's build one to find out!

Set Up the Sand Dunes

The first thing we need in our desert is sand.
We can make piles of sand called dunes.

Sand dunes look like hills. Some are very big. Others are small.

Dunes are formed when wind blows sand into piles. They change shape as the wind keeps blowing the sand around.

Some dunes have **steep** sides.

Add the Rocks

Our sand looks great! But deserts are made of more than just sand. Let's add some rocks to our desert, too.

Many desert **landscapes** are rocky instead of just sandy.

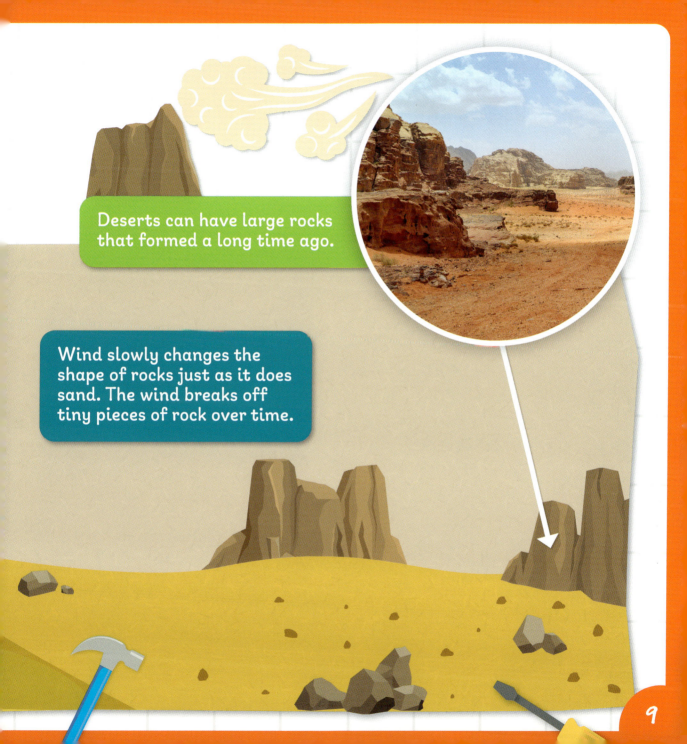

Deserts can have large rocks that formed a long time ago.

Wind slowly changes the shape of rocks just as it does sand. The wind breaks off tiny pieces of rock over time.

Welcome the Weather

We've already seen some wind in our desert. But what other types of weather can a desert have?

During the day, deserts can be some of the hottest places on Earth.

At night, the **temperature** changes. Deserts can become freezing cold when the sun goes down.

Deserts are very dry. They get almost no rain.

Bring In the Storms

Next, we need to add the most **extreme** desert weather of all. Let's make some storms!

Strong winds can make giant clouds of sand and dust. These clouds are called dust storms or sandstorms.

Dust storms can be taller than 1,000 giraffes standing on top of one another!

Sandstorms move quickly. They can carry lots of sand very far.

13

Place the Plants

Plants need water to live. Because there's very little rain, we need special plants to put in our dry desert.

Cactus plants can hold water for a very long time. They can **survive** while waiting for rain in the desert.

A cactus holds water in its **trunk**.

There are many different kinds of cactuses. Some are short. Others grow tall like trees.

Invite the Animals

Like most plants, a lot of animals can't live in deserts. These dry places have little food. But some animals have **adapted** to survive.

Sidewinder snakes hide in the sand. This helps them sneak up on **prey**.

Camels can survive without food for days. They live off the fat in the humps on their backs until they can find something to eat.

Vultures can see very well. This helps them spot food while flying high in the sky.

17

Open an Oasis

While most of our big desert is dry, we can add a place that has water. Let's build an oasis.

An oasis is an area in a desert that has lots of water and plants.

An oasis forms when water from deep underground comes up to the **surface**.

Animals can get water from an oasis.

19

Find Another Desert

We made an amazing hot desert. But did you know that deserts can be cold, too? Let's find a cold desert . . .

Cold deserts often have hot summers and cold winters. Sometimes, they get snow. But they are still deserts because they are very dry.

There are not many plants in cold deserts, just like in hot deserts.

You might find penguins, camels, or snow leopards in cold deserts.

Make Your Own Environment

Desert environments are incredible! They can have awesome animals, tall sand dunes, and giant storms. Now, it's time to build your own environment! You could draw it, paint it, or write about it. What do you want to put in your desert?

Will you make a hot desert or a cold desert?

Which plants or animals will live there?

What will the weather be like in your desert?

Glossary

adapted changed over time to fit the environment

environments the different parts of our world in which people, animals, and plants live

extreme much beyond what is normal or expected

landscapes areas of land

prey animals that are hunted by other animals for food

steep having a sharp slope

surface the top part of something

survive to stay alive

temperature how hot or cold something is

trunk the thick, main stem of certain plants

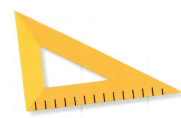

Index